I Think I Have Fairies
In My Garden

Alexandra Grose

Balboa Press books may be ordered through booksellers or by contacting:

Balboa Press
A Division of Hay House
1663 Liberty Drive
Bloomington, IN 47403
www.balboapress.com.au
AU TFN: 1 800 844 925 (Toll Free inside Australia)
AU Local: 0283 107 086 (+61 2 8310 7086 from outside Australia)

ISBN: 978-1-5043-2180-8 (sc)
ISBN: 978-1-5043-2179-2 (e)

Print information available on the last page.

Balboa Press rev. date: 06/20/2020

BALBOA PRESS
A DIVISION OF HAY HOUSE

I Think I Have Fairies
In My Garden

Hello children,

My name is Nanna and I'm a writer. I like to tell stories.

I live a long way from your place. It's cold where

I live and sometimes it even snows.

But where I live has beautiful flowers, once

winter is over and spring arrives.

My garden is as pretty as a picture, in spring time,

when the bluebells and roses are in bloom.

I think I have fairies in my garden.

Whenever my grand-daughter, Kristelle, comes for a visit, she picks the roses and puts them on the garden table. The roses always disappear. I reckon the fairies take the roses and use the petals, for bedsheets. It would be very soft and snuggly, sleeping between rose petal sheets.

Not far from where I live, there's a place called 'Fairy Bower.' It's in the middle of a rain forest that has lots of trees, with a narrow little path, which passes through the centre. There's a waterfall, near the end of the trail, where the fairies have their shower. I heard if you go there at night, you might just see the fairies, dancing in the moonlight.

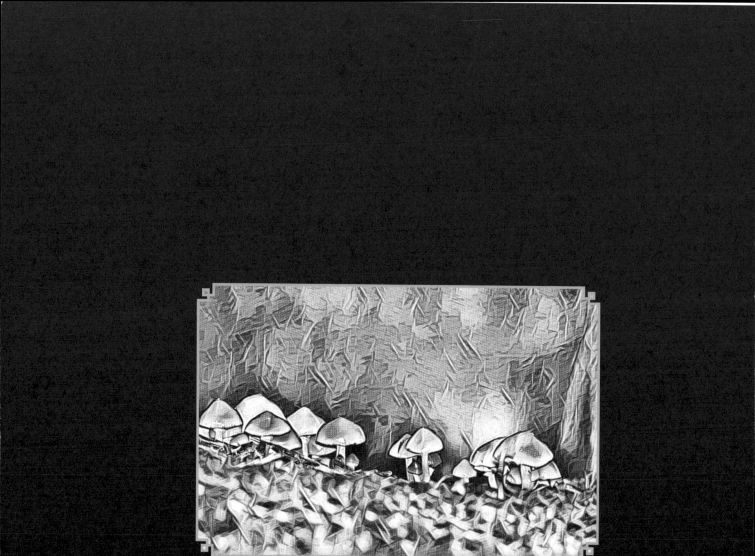

Kristelle and I didn't see any fairies, the night we went, but we did find

Fairy City. All was quiet that night. I think we went too late and all the

fairies were asleep. Either that, or they heard us coming and they hid,

keeping oh so quiet and staying out of sight. Fairies are very shy you know.

Sometimes Kristelle sits in the garden, waiting for the fairies to come out and play. One day, Kristelle was almost certain she saw one, but when the fairy saw her, it quickly hid. Kristelle looked all through the garden, but never found the fairy. Fairies are very quick and very good at hiding amongst the flowers.

Over my garden, is a streetlight and Ollie the owl likes to sit on it.

He's also watching and waiting, for the fairies to come out and play,

in my garden. Ollie's hoping to catch a fairy, but only because he

wants to eat it. I expect fairies would be really tasty and sweet, since

all they drink is flower nectar. No wonder Ollie wants to catch one.

This is our dog, Soxx. I call her Miss Spoilty-Soxx, because whenever we go for a drive, Soxx sits on the front seat of the car, while Poppy sits in the back. She is very spoilt.

Soxx doesn't like Ollie. She knows, Ollie's after the fairies. Whenever Soxx sees Ollie, she runs up to him, barking loudly and chases him away. There's plenty of worms in the garden Ollie could eat, so he won't go hungry.

Now children, the reason I'm telling you this story, is I have something important, which I think you should know.

What I want you to know is; I wasn't always a writer.

When I was a little bit older than you, my teacher said I wasn't clever enough to be a writer. She said I'd be better working in a laundromat, washing people's dirty clothes and I believed her, so I never became a writer until I was very old.

Beautiful children, if someone tells you, you aren't clever enough to be what you want to be, when you grow up, don't you believe them!

When people tell you, you aren't clever enough, you believe in yourself and work hard to prove them wrong.

The End!

Written by Alexandra Grose

Printed in the United States
By Bookmasters